A Voice in the Void

The Paradox of Life

JustFiction Edition

Imprint

Any brand names and product names mentioned in this book are subject to trademark, brand or patent protection and are trademarks or registered trademarks of their respective holders. The use of brand names, product names, common names, trade names, product descriptions etc. even without a particular marking in this work is in no way to be construed to mean that such names may be regarded as unrestricted in respect of trademark and brand protection legislation and could thus be used by anyone.

Cover image: www.ingimage.com

Publisher:
JustFiction! Edition
is a trademark of
International Book Market Service Ltd., member of OmniScriptum Publishing Group
17 Meldrum Street, Beau Bassin 71504, Mauritius

Printed at: see last page
ISBN: 978-620-2-48973-7

Rami's maternal aunt, who was present at his birth, recounted Rami's entrance to the world hammering into his mind the doom he brought to his mother. She described the horrific atmosphere of his birthday as the following: *your mother had to have a cesarean to deliver you. The operating table was covered with blood all over. When the anesthetic effect receded, she slowly opened her eyes and screamed out with horror and the doctors had to cover her mouth to stop her from yelling.*

Rami was not only the cause of his mother's death, but he was also considered a bad omen to the Alwadi village. His birthday coincided with one of the most devastating floods recorded in the history of natural disasters in the country.

The Alwadi was a prosperous agricultural village set in a fertile valley. In the east, it was fenced with a giant mountain chain called the Ketay Mountain Chain and in the southwest it was bordered by a mighty river called the Mero River. The village was overlooked by a massive volcanic dome. The dome's position was so spectacular that the village folks dubbed it "the Giant Umbrella". It was named so for it acted as a natural shield against morning hours' sunlight.

The village was known for its vast fertile floodplain where various cash crops were grown. Sesame and cotton were the most important crops cultivated in the vast plain extending along the eastern bank. The cultivation fields were fed with complex irrigation channels running throughout the fields. The village was also famous for its riches in livestock. The sheer geographical location made the Alwadi a top breeder of cattle and one of the biggest producers of cash crops.

The Alwadi village never knew any hardship, but lives of prosperity, peace, and serenity. But on that very day of Rami's birth, as if nature conspired to lay the blame on him, disaster struck.

This prosperous, serene Alwadi was swallowed by a catastrophic flood when the Mero River overflowed its banks and tore down the embankment along the giant Ketay Mountain. The flood devoured many districts of the Fellahia city. The Alwadi was the first region to succumb to the furious murky water. The mud huts dissolved like pieces of biscuits dipped in hot water. Bodies floated like plastic bags on the dusty water. The scale of the destruction was beyond imagination. The unwary dwellers were taken by a total surprise and made a desperate scrambling up the cliff of the Ketay Mountain towering the Alwadi.

The sky was overcast with dark looming clouds heralding heavy rain. Soon it began to rain. It descended in large sharp drops and was accompanied by a violent storm with thunder and lightning. It seemed nature braced itself to wipe out Alwadi once and for all!

Amid the floods Rami was wrapped in a towel and moved towards the cliff where the terror stricken survivors were huddling together plunged in chaos. Eventually, after whole day of relentless torrents, just the second hour of the new day the rain gave in.

In the break of the day light, the survivors opened their eyes to utter destruction and then they veered their faces to Rami, the baby who killed his mother and who brought the doom on the village.

Rami was raised by his aunt and her husband who was a truck driver. They had two children: Sarah and Mejid who loved their cousin, Rami, very much. They thought he was their brother. Rami's foster family lived in a rental house on the outskirts of Shergania, a densely populated suburb towards the northeast from the Alwadi village. They shifted there twelve years after the floods when the local municipality decreed that the Alwadi would be relocated to Shergania.

The government compensated the displaced households with handsome amounts of money for the relocation costs. Besides, plots were allotted freely to build the resettlement. Most of the families constructed their own houses. Only few of them took rental houses and so did Rami's foster family. Rami's uncle Kedos, instead of constructing a new house in the allotted plot, he decided to take a rental house, a proposition which Rami's aunt, Tayiba strongly opposed.

One evening Tyiba and her husband had a serious argument.

"Are we going to live like this forever?" Complained Tayiba.

"Like what?" Inquired Kedos.

"Everybody is constructing their houses!" Affirmed Tayiba.

"We are not everybody and everybody's problem is not our problem! We do what is convenient for us!!" Denied Kedos.

"So what is your plan?" Demanded Tayiba.

After taking a long deep breathe, Kedos said, "Last night I talked to a friend of mine. A close friend. He works for a private car-sale company........."

"What are you talking about?" Interrupted Tayiba.

"About my plan!! We are going to buy a pick-up truck!" Said Kedos bluntly.

"A pick-up truck!! What for?" She said surprisingly.

The man paused for a moment and then evasively said, "I have already met an expert in second-hand cars. He has found me a used pick-up truck in perfect condition. The car is now under further inspection and I already paid the initial installment"

"What do you mean by *initial installment*? You did that even without sharing your plan with me!!" Shouted the woman.

"I am sharing it with you now! After all, it is for the betterment of our family!" Consoled Kedos.

"I see!! That is why you didn't want to construct the house!! After all, where is the money to buy a vehicle?" Tayiba posed suspiciously.

"Don't worry!! My friend has convinced the company that I would repay the loan in 32 monthly installments." The man reassured.

"But we cannot afford to risk whatever little money we have for luxury goods!!" Grudged Tayiba.

"A pick-up truck is not a luxury!! We are going to make money out of it!! And you are well aware that I am fed up of working under others. I always longed for my own car" Kedos said excitedly.

Kedos was obsessed with the idea of buying a pick-up truck. He considered buying a car on a hire purchase was the only way to fulfill his dream. After a long heated argument, finally Tayiba surrendered and it was settled that Kedos would purchase the vehicle.

Before, Rami's foster family shifted to Shergania, life was easy in Alwadi. His aunt and her husband were happy. His aunt was a good housewife. Apart from housework, she used to sell vegetables to supplement the household's average income. But when they moved to Shergania, life became difficult and hard. The household expenditure gradually began to put a strain on the family's income. Just like nowadays, at that time quality schooling meant private, so Rami's aunt and her husband somehow managed to send the kids to a private school. Now, Sara and Majid needed school fees. Rami was already in the sixth grade, but he didn't have the aptitude for academic subjects. After school he used to spend most of the time practicing musical instruments.

He nurtured the love for music since early childhood. Their neighbor and a friend of the family, Arkadi taught him how to play musical instruments. Arkadi was a retired conductor. He had spent a lifetime teaching music. Rami kept pestering him to teach him playing musical instruments. Arkadi sensed that Rami had a natural aptitude for music. Every now and then he would say that Rami would be a good artist in future, an idea which Rami's family frowned upon especially his uncle. Kedos always worried himself sick about Rami's carelessness with school.

"I'm worried about the future of this kid," complained Kedos.

A complaint to which Mr. Arkadi replied, "Don't worry, the boy's future is written on his face. He will be a great musician!"

For a patient and calm man like Kedos, it was an unusual to feel that way. But the fact is that he was obviously exhausted with Rami's increasing obsession for music. Kedos thought the boy's poor performance in school was attributable to his devotion to music. Kedos was right. Rami's devotion to music left him with very little free time to study.

Over time, Rami gradually became mad about music. Music had become an obsession with him to the extent that Kedos and his wife confessed that they felt as if they were living with sound and that sound didn't make any sense to them. Rami was a sort of music maniac. He moved in an atmosphere which wasn't like theirs at all. He was wrapped up in some cloud, some fire, and some vision of his own. He was an enigma to them and there wasn't any way for anyone to understand his inner voice.

At the same time, he wasn't really a man yet. He was still a child. And they had to watch him out in all kinds of ways. For a long time he had been lying to his family about his schooling. Every now and then he used to bunk off school and make his way home and sneak into Arkadi's house to practice musical instruments. One time, the school headmaster summoned Kedos to discuss Rami's truancy and his repeated absences from school.

Henceforth, his uncle would closely monitor him in all kinds of ways. The boy was strictly forbidden from touching any musical instrument and evening curfews were imposed on him. But it was a matter of time before he would relapse into his habit.

Soon Rami discovered another place where he could get access to musical instruments. It was mid-term examination period and he missed two exams. He went to attend music lessons given by a voluntary white woman.

This day when he came in, his uncle showed him a letter which bore the school seal. Then he asked him where he had been. And he finally got it out of him that he had been with musicians and other characters, in a white woman's apartment. And this shocked Rami's foster parents and they started screaming at the boy furiously. Kedos complained bitterly of the sacrifice they were making to give him a decent education. The silence of the next few days must have been louder than the sound of all the music ever played since time began.

That was only a part of Rami's early childhood history. The other side of his childhood life was worse than the disappointment he caused his family due to his obsession with music. When he was young, he was labeled as a wayward and notoriously troublesome child. The neighbors bred a very bad feeling for him. They thought he was an evil child and a constant threat to their children.

Now and then the neighbors would storm Rami's family house with complaints against him as soon as his aunt returned home. His aunt was tall and slender woman with a freckled face. Outwardly, she maintained a smiling face, but hidden behind this smiling face were a streak of cruelty and violent temper. Besides, she was a strict disciplinarian. Any infraction didn't go unpunished. Sometimes, she would do terrible things when she was in a temper. Anything which came to her hand was used as a weapon: a ladle, a plate, a shoe etcetera.

One day, she hurled a kitchen stool onto Rami after discovering that he had sneaked into a neighbor's house to steal eggs. Another day, she struck him with a ladle on his head for hitting a neighbor's son. This time, Rami was seriously injured and was taken to a clinic. This incident brought a serious clash between Tayiba and her husband. Tayiba believed in the dictum: punishment and discipline go hand in hand. She did not know that it makes the child stubborn and cynic. Kedos was a sane person. He believed advice and instruction make the children understand their mistakes and try to rectify them. Tayiba was adamant that children had to be punished physically. On one occasion Tayiba had a hot argument with her friend Razga regarding family related issues. Razga was an old woman. She was a close friend of Tayiba. Tayiba first met her in the market. Razga like Tayiba used to sell vegetables.

When asked why she was too harsh with children, Tayiba replied, "The only way to straighten a stubborn child is a stick."

Rami's cousins and their father always sided with Rami and were dragged into any quarrel to defend him. They shared with him deep seated resentments against Tayiba's aggressive attitude.

Tayiba's cruelty became a common gossip in the neighborhood. But she was too stubborn to admit that she was harsh, instead she tightened the grip on Rami and his cousins.

In spite of this aggressive tendency, Tayiba was admired for her industry and perseverance. She always tried to instill in her family the love for hard work. And she was never tired of repeating this phrase: hard work is the only path to self-advancement!

Rami called his aunt by her name as his uncle did and his cousins followed him. His uncle Kedos was tall, dark and handsome man with a very long moustache and bushy beard punctuated with strands of grey hair. Kedos was surprisingly calm and kind! He always spoke in a husky whisper. He never raised his hand to hit anyone in the family. But seldom he would be at home. Sometimes, he would stay away for several days and even for weeks, especially when he was engaged in cross-border transit.

Although Kedos was a good man, some of his habits earned him a bad reputation. He was described as an uncouth and drunken man. Tayiba believed the same.

Kedos had never been concerned about his appearance. His hands and clothes were always stained with oil and petrol. A lingering smell of machine oil always emanated from him. Rami never liked sharing with him the same serving dish.

Kedos was a chain smoker. Sometimes, he sniffed tobacco when he ran out of cigarettes. His bedroom was always messy. The floor was covered with a litter of cigarette butts and disposed of tobacco. The room always stunk of stale tobacco and cigarette smoke. He never thought of using ashtrays.

For years, his wife had been tolerating his behavior. But now she became increasingly impatient with him. Particularly, now the kids were grown up and she didn't want her husband to display any bad behavior in front of the kids.

"I am sick and tired of your cigarettes and tobacco!" I am not going to put up with your filthy habit anymore." Tayiba complained one fine morning.

A complaint, to which, Kedos responded with a nod of disgust.

As time passed by, Kedos indulged himself in even more worse habit: alcohol. He gradually became addicted to a traditionally brewed strong alcoholic drink called *katikala*. In spite of these habits, Kedos was a devoted family man. He always made sure that the kids were taken care of.

After Kedos acquired the car, many welcome and positive changes were seen in the family. First, Tayiba stopped going to sell vegetables. She started doing household chores and helping children in their studies. Financially, they were improving, so did their living standard. Besides, Kedos was spending a large chunk of his time with family which was rare earlier.

Kedos transported goods and passengers. Most of the time, he shuttled between Shergania and the neighboring villages.

Although, things worked out quite well for Tyaiba and her husband, there was not much saving. Most of the money had to go to settle the loan. According to the deal, every month Kedos had to pay 3 percent.

Now Tayiba's perception in her assessment of the situation gradually began to change in favor of her husband's decision. She began to realize that the car was worth the risk.

Two years elapsed since Kedos had bought the car and so far everything was going on well. The family looked more stable than ever before. At this time, Tayiba was pregnant with her third child. Sara and Mejid started school and Rami was shuttling between music classes and school. Sometimes he used to fetch Mejid from school when Tayiba was busy. Sara was a grown up girl and she could go to school by herself.

One hot afternoon, while Rami was walking Majid home, from the distance he saw a crowd gathered around their house. Most of them were men and women of the neighborhood. At first glance, he thought his aunt had given birth. As he got closer, however, he saw pensive looks on the people's faces. He sensed something was wrong and he assumed it had to do with his aunt. Anxious and perplexed, he pushed his way through the crowd and immediately rushed into the living room and found Arkadi and Sara sitting side by side. Arkadi was talking to Sarah in a low, sad voice.

Rami cried out, "uncle Arkadi what is going on?? Where is my aunt?"

Arkadi raised his head slowly and said, "Calm down, calm down everything is ok!!"

"What do you mean everything is Ok! Tell me where is my…..." Rami cried out.

"She went to see your uncle. He is having a small problem with his car!" Interrupted a trembling voice.

It was Razga Tayiba's friend. The tone of her voice sent a wave of shock throughout Rami's body. Razga made a palpable attempt to hide what had really happened, but it was obvious that it was something serious. She sat down to conceal the fact she was trembling.

Arkadi stood up and moved towards Razga and said, "How is he?"

"It was terrible, but he is lucky that he was rushed to the hospital!" Said Razga.

"Yeah, indeed it was an unfortunate accident!" Condemned Arkadi.

Arkadi walked towards the door and glanced back at Rami and said, "I will come back soon."

Rami knew Arkadi was going to the hospital and so he followed him.

"Where are going you?" Asked Razga.

'I am going with him!" Rami said in a trembling voice.

"No, you stay with your cousins!" Objected Razga. "You can't leave them alone!"

"What do you mean you stay with your cousins? I want to see my uncle!! I will go even on my own!" Rami cried out.

"We are all going to the hospital to see him!" Interrupted Arkadi.

Then they immediately tramped their way to the hospital. They took Sara and Mejid along with them. Arkadi carried Mejid on his shoulder. As they hurried their way to hospital, the heat of the afternoon sun seared their faces and their bodies were soaked in sweat. Everybody was silent except for the tramp of their feet.

By the time they arrived in the hospital, Kedos was still in the emergency room lying supine with his eyes closed. His head and both legs were all bandaged up and he was put on a drip. Rami was about to faint at the sight of blood being transfused into his uncle. The nurses were busy attending to the other injured and they seemed unconcerned by their presence.

Tayiba was sitting on a chair beside her husband's bed; her face looked strained and a little unnerved.

"What is his condition?" Asked Arkadi.

"The injuries are serious and he lost a lot of blood!" Said Tayiba in a low voice.

Then Arkadi took one of the nurses aside and whispered, "How serious are the injuries, nurse?"

"We assume his legs are fractured. We will take him for an X-ray in two days," said the nurse.

After some time the doctors asked everybody to leave, except Tayiba. On their way home they met one of the passengers who escaped with only minor scratches, and he described the accident as very terrible. He was in Kedos's car when a heavy truck slammed into their car from behind.

After three days, the x-ray results confirmed Kedos had serious bone fractures and was transferred to a bone hospital.

Kedos spent a long period of hospitalization. Tayiba had to shuttle between her house and the hospital until her husband was discharged. It took him about three months to recover from his injuries. This created a vacuum in the family.

The accident put Kedos off work for life. He had his both legs amputated. Henceforth, he was to be confined to a wheelchair. And this cost Tayiba the burden of bringing up three children single-handedly. Besides, Kedos's impairment plunged every member of the family into huge emotional disturbance. Kedos who was once energetic and dynamic man, now reduced to an invalid monster.

One fine evening while the family was having dinner, gathered around the dining table as usual, Kedos's amputated legs caught Mejid's attention. This time, Kedos was caught at a bad moment, he was wearing cut-off pants. He had seldom revealed his impairment, especially in front of his kids. On his wheelchair he just looked like a half-finished dummy. All eyes were fixed on Kedos who was really in a sorry sight.

While they were all waiting for Tayiba to set the dining table, Mejid cautiously reached his right hand to his father's knees and said, "Where are your legs? Dad!"

Kedos stroke Mejid's hair, smiled faintly and said, "I left them in the hospital!"

"Why?? When are you going to get them back?" Asked Mejid innocently.

"You will get them for me when you grow up!" Said Kedos ironically.

"You naughty boy come here! Don't disturb your father!" Interrupted Tayiba.

As time dragged by, life became tough on Tayiba. She worked herself too hard to take care of her husband and her three children. To supplement her meager income, she started cleaning at night. She also hired Rami out to a poultry farm.

Rami's main job at the poultry was to run errands. Usually, he hung about the farm ready for anything that any of the workers would set him to. Sometimes, he had to look after the chicken along with other workmates. He helped them watering and feeding the chicken. He also cleaned the droppings. In the workplace, they nicknamed him "Bitza" meaning feeding bottle; partly because he sucked milk through a feeding bottle when he was an infant, and partly because he had the habit of sucking his thumb.

Though the workmates were nice and friendly, for nearly one month Rami distanced himself from them. He was always cautious and suspicious of people around him and as soon as he finished his work, he rushed into his room and lay down on his bed pondering. During night time, he played the *rabbaba* to himself. Sometimes, he used to play into late night and at times he used to sing at the top of his voice.

As time dragged on, he gradually got used to the work environment and the people around. A good working relationship was nurtured between Rami and his workmates, particularly, between him and one of the boys who was close to him in age. His name was Sheboun.

Although Sheboun looked far mature for his age, he had a lot of annoying habits to foil the good side of his personality. He was downright rude, reckless, and bothersome, among other things.

One afternoon while Rami was playing his *rabbaba* sitting under a "Mexic" tree, Sheboun approached him and asked, "Yesterday I listened to the melody of your *rabbaba*. It was hauntingly sad! Very sad!"

"It is true." Rami acknowledged.

"Why was that?" Sheboun inquired.

"The world is full of sad tunes!" Rami explained.

"You live with your parents? Sheboun asked.

"No, I live with my aunt," Rami replied.

"And what about your parents?" Sheboun asked.

"I don't know my parents. My mother died while giving birth to me and as for my father, I was told he disappeared two months after my mother's death!" Rami replied.

"Aha, another destitute!!" Sheboun smiled wryly.

"What do you mean?" Rami asked.

"Before I came to this damn place, I used to work in a tobacconist's," Sheboun commenced his story without Rami's invitation.

"I was a product of a broken home. My mother sold alcohol to support us. My father- well that son-of-bitch left us when I was five years old," he sneered.

"My mother got involved in dirty activities with various men and left me without a curfew. I came home and went as pleased. Sometimes I would spend nights out," he continued.

"What the heck?" Rami muttered.

After a long deep breathe Sheboun said, "One day a man, one of the regular customers, talked to my mother that he had found me a job"

He paused for a moment, and then continued, "The man convinced my mother that the job would keep me away from bad habits. The next morning the man came to our house and took me along with him and brought me here. Now it has been six months' time since I started work here in this shitty place. It is a matter of time until I get the fuck out of this shithole."

After he had finished his story, he breathed deeply and reached to the pocket of his pants and drew out a red pack of cigarettes. He lit a cigarette and after having two deep puffs, he said, "Have you ever smoked?"

"No!" Rami nodded.

"I started smoking when I was only twelve and since then these babies have been my buddies!" Sheboun said starring amusingly at the cigarettes in the pack.

"And sadly, I started alcohol before I was born. I'm an offspring of alcohol addicted mother who couldn't stop drinking even in her pregnancy!" he continued.

Rami was silent in a state of shock as Sheboun narrated his woeful story.

"My mother also smokes," Sheboun added.

"What??" Rami startled.

Sheboun laughed wryly and said, "You should have seen your face! You look like you are clouted with a brick!!"

Then he held the pack in front of Rami and asked, "Do you read?"

"I quit school when I was a six grader." Rami replied.

"(*Real cigarettes for real smokers!! But watch out, smoking kills*)!" He read the ad on the back of the pack.

"If it kills then why you smoke?" Rami enquired.

"A bloody good question!!" he sneered. "You just taste it first, and then only you will tell why?"

Then he drew on his cigarette and blew out a stream of a smoke and then swaggered his way into his room looking very pleased with himself. Before entering his room, he glanced back and smiled faintly.

As he slid into his room, Rami closed his eyes and had a deep breath and then pondered over Sheboun's words for a while. Sheboun's story shook every nerve in his body. The story heavily weighed on Rami's mind for the next several days.

The relationship between Rami and Sheboun gradually deepened. Rami soon found himself thrown into the company of the most fascinating person he had ever met in his life. He admired his boldness and frankness. Besides, Sheboun's happy and carefree attitude stunned Rami. As time passed by, Rami found himself seeking Sheboun's company. He would look around for him.

One late Friday afternoon, while Rami was playing his *rabbaba* as usual, Sheboun came and sat beside him and started rocking his head to the tune of Rami's instrument.

Rami couldn't contain his laughter as he saw Sheboun swaying his hip clumsily. The *rabbaba* fell off his grab as he dissolved into deep laughter. Sheboun started laughing along with him. When they both split their sides with laughter, Rami resumed playing his instrument even more enthusiastically.

No sooner had he started to play the *rabbaba* than Sheboun grabbed Rami's left hand, interrupting him, "Play me a song?"

"Play what?" Rami smirked.

Sheboun hummed a tune of a familiar song and then asked, "Recognize it?"

"I remember the song" Rami replied.

It was a difficult piece and Rami had to try it several times until he got the right tempo.

Sheboun was getting impatient and kept repeating, "Hey dude, what's up?"

After few rounds of rehearsal, Rami was finally able to play it and Sheboun began singing in unison with him.

"It is my all-time favorite song…… a pleasant reminder of my childhood! Don't stop it" said Sheboun tapping his feet.

"Really!" Rami nodded.

Then Rami played it again and again as Sheboun continued singing along with him.

"Fantastic!! That is really great of you!" Sheboun complimented clapping his hands excitedly.

Then all of a sudden he rose to his feet and said, "Accompany me, I have to see somebody!!"

Rami stared up in disbelief and said, "Where to buddy?"

"To the den of debauchery!" Sheboun sneered.

"What?? What are you talking about?" Rami asked in disbelief. The tone, as much as the words, came as a shock to Rami.

Without saying any further word, Sheboun bent forward and held Rami by his forearm and then said, "Come on get up! Get up, you lazy musician! You do know life is much more than being able to play a *rabbaba* out of tune! You think your rabbaba is the center of the universe!"

"Let's push off!" He yelled excitedly.

Rami was very reluctant to go anywhere, but Sheboun really wanted him to go with him. Sheboun softened the matter by saying that he was going to meet his girl, who wished to see him so much. He said she lived in Juzran, a small town a bit far from the work place.

Eventually, he agreed to accompany him. They slipped out of the farm compound before others awoke and took the back lane which led to the nearby scattered Mexic tree bush. They walked along a ravine until they melted into a far distance.

On their way, Sheboun turned towards Rami and said, "I am glad to have your company!"

Rami stared at him and grinned.

13

"You see those selfish old rascals; they leave all work to us in the weekends and go to tickle their wives!! I hate them all!!" Sheboun snarled. "They can't continue milking us like that. Now let them find it."

Rami just listened as Sheboun kept grudging.

Being engaged in deep discussion, the two boys made to the main road even without being aware of how far they had come out. They walked along the road hoping they would get a lift, but there were no vehicles on sight. After walking for nearly half an hour along the road, they turned to the left and took a foot lane.

They continued walking oblivious to the surrounding, until they eventually awakened to the hazy Juzran houses appearing in the distance. They were delighted at the mere sight of Juzran, ignoring the long distance ahead of them. A barren landscape extended endlessly as the setting sun cast an orange glow over the little town.

Evening was falling by the time they reached Kadugli, a slum in the outskirts of Juzran and one of the sleaziest quarters of the town infamous for having one way in and no way out.

From the distance, they were welcomed by the hubbub of the nauseous slum life. The smell of alcohol faintly wafted through the air. Rami grew anxious and nervous as they walked along the narrow, semi-dark streets which split the shanty, mud-brick houses. Now, it was early evening and the children were still running around.

"By the way, you should have no trouble in tasting the manly brews!" Sheboun fortified Rami. "Big boy pants on...... leave your baby's bottle at home!"

"Yeah...yeah!!" Rami nodded in agreement, although in reality he was uncomfortable.

"Got what I mean?" Sheboun continued. "Be a man!"

Finally, they halted at a gate loosely hinged on a massive mud wall. Sheboun pushed open the old rusting iron gate and beckoned Rami to follow him in. They passed through a thatched porch and entered into a spacious room ahead of them on the right side.

The moment they entered the room Rami was struck by a nauseous smell of mix of cigarette smoke and stale alcohol. The entire place wore a festive, but rather disorderly atmosphere. The floor was littered with empty bottles and cigarette butts. Most of the tables were occupied by customers of various age groups. All were men. Some of them sprawled in their chairs and sipped at their drinks. Others played cards raving at each other. A deafeningly loud music burst out of twin woofers each fixed to a pillar standing on either side of the doorway. Clouds of cigarette smoke rose spirally in the beams produced by two bare tungsten bulbs dangling from the ceiling.

Sheboun, who was a head taller than Rami, looked down at his friend and inhaled the stale air then smiled proudly, "This is the real entertainment!"

Everyone seemed oblivious of their arrival and to the noise around. Sheboun went straightaway to the adjoining room leaving Rami in this mad place to his own.

Now Rami had the time to think about what to do next. He stood in a corner perplexedly studying the house. Then all of a sudden he was startled by an unfamiliar voice calling, "Bitza! Bitza! Come over here!" It was a hefty woman standing on the doorway of the adjoining room. She was holding a drink in her right hand. As Rami approached her, the woman put her left arm across his shoulders and took him inside.

The room was calmer and tidier than the first. Rami was seated at a couch beside a middle-aged man who was drinking beer. Sheboun was sitting on the opposite end with his left hand rested on the shoulders of a young girl. A bottle of liquor was placed on a table in front of him.

Sheboun glanced around and gestured for Rami to hang on for a second. He sounded as if he was engaged in a meaty conversation with the girl. The man beside Rami was glancing at a magazine while sipping his drink. He was oblivious to what was going on around him. Rami leaned back in the couch and began glancing around the room. Then, all of a sudden his eyes rested on a white cat which was curling on the floor. With nothing to do, he started teasing the cat.

The man glanced at Rami, shook his head and continued with his magazine with a sneer. Then he started smiling ambivalently with his eyes glued to the magazine. Rami suddenly stopped teasing the cat and folded his arms and started humming while tapping his legs on the floor.

"*I annoyed him*!!" He thought. Out of the corner of his eye, he saw the man closing the magazine.

After a while the man turned around and tossed the magazine to Rami and slurred, "Hey kid, so you are playing with the pussycat, huh?......here's a real pussy for you.....feast your eyes!"

Rami looked at him confusedly. "*A mere stream of drunken gibberish!*" he reflected.

The man leaned forward, tapped Rami on his shoulder and then, pointing towards Sheboun, he slurred, "You see they are enjoying alone together. You might as well have a treat with these!"

Then the man grabbed his bottle from the table and staggered doorway.

Rami couldn't understand for the life of him what the man meant by "A REAL PUSSY!" Without paying much attention to the cover page, he just glanced at the magazine and when he saw what was in the magazine, he almost jumped out of his skin. A woman he had never seen before was as naked as the day she was born. She was on all fours while a big naked man was glued to her buttocks.

"What kind of a daft joke is this?" Rami muttered as he studied the pictures. He was startled from his business with the barks of Sheboun: "HEY BITZA, GET YOUR ASS OVER HERE...... We are done for now!!"

Rami hauled himself up and walked over and sat down in the chair opposite.

Didi, referring to the girl, Sheboun said, "This is my friend Bitza. He is a musical prodigy. Should have heard him play his *rabbaba*!"

Then he turned around and said, "She is my broad!!"

She softly said, "Hallo, Mozart" and smiled.

Rami extended his hand and shyly said, "Hallo."

When she leaned forward to greet him, Rami could see her sizable round mounds jiggling inside her loose transparent blouse.

Sheboun rose to his feet with a cigarette hung from his lips and said, "**Sadri**, one more cup for the musician!"

After a while, a hefty woman, the very woman who brought Rami in, came waddling towards them. She brought two cups and a bottle of soda water. She placed the cups and the soda on the table and sunk into a big wooden chair. After chatting for a while the woman poured out *katikala* liquor and added some soda.

Rami's eyes rolled over the brimming cups. He couldn't believe he was doing this. While he was struggling with his conscience, Sheboun's words rang in his head, "*Big boy pants on...... leave your baby's bottle at home....... Be a man!*"

Sheboun raised his cup and said, "To the future of our prodigy."

16

The two women stared at Rami, smiled faintly and repeated in unison, "To the future of our prodigy."

Then everybody gulped down their drinks, but Rami.

After gulping down his drink, Sheboun glared furiously at Rami and gestured for him to drink.

Rami stared down at the cup, hesitated a little, and then drained the glass in one gulp.

Sheboun punched the air in excitement and yelled, "That is it!! Now you are initiated into the world of sanity! The world is your oyster now!"

Rami grimaced at the bitter taste. His throat was burning as the drink went down. After a while, a shaft of numbing sensation ran throughout his body and thick foams kept amassing in his mouth forcing him to spit repeatedly.

"Where did you pick this sorry thing?" Sadri whispered to Sheboun and then she gave a short, derisive laugh.

Sheboun glared at her and then smiled at Rami reassuringly.

Rami gave a sheepish grin and passed it off as a minor discomfort in the stomach.

For the rest of the rounds, Rami would take his drink only in sips and everybody outpaced him. He found the taste of the drink very repellent and kept diluting it with coke. As the night passed by, bottles kept coming and the mood of the feast alternated moments of drinking with moments of excitement accompanied by dance. Rami was silent, lost in thoughts. Sometimes, he tapped his feet to the low music wafting from the opposite corner of the room. Now and then Sadri would poke him and say, "Hey young man, cheer up!"

It was some time before Rami's inhibition turned into a thin air. After four or five rounds he could only remember he was blissed out and started smiling. He started tapping his fingers on the table and hummed along with the music frantically.

Sheboun hauled out of his chair and dragged Rami humorously to the dance floor. They joined hands and began dancing round. Soon everybody joined. Sheboun and his girl held each other closely and danced slowly. Rami felt a queer, mortifying sensation between his legs watching Sadri move her massive wiggly buttocks. "What the heck!" he gasped in a choked voice. In a frenzy of excitement, he made a dart for the table and drained his cup in just one gulp and lit a cigarette. They stayed up drinking and dancing into late night.

17

In the middle of the revelry, Rami felt a piercing jolt in his stomach followed by a wave of nausea and relentless whirl. He was pissed as a newt. The next thing he knew, he was lying on a couch covered with puke. He couldn't believe this could happen to him. He leaped out of the couch and looked around for Sheboun. The house appeared completely deserted. A deafening silence fell everywhere, except for the soft ticks coming from around the spacious room. Rami rubbed his hands wearily over his eyes and squinted in an attempt to locate the source. A rectangular clock was fixed to the wall. Its hands said: 11:15.

"Gosh!" Rami whispered and staggered his way to the toilet.

When he crawled back, he ghosted around looking for Sheboun. He was nowhere to be seen. After a while, he heard heavy snores coming out of the next door. He went straightaway and slowly pushed the door open and peeped inside. When he stepped in, he stumbled upon a large clumsy figure lying on a mattress spread on the floor. It was Sadri. She was lying in a prone position buck naked. Her colossal buttocks stuck out like a gigantic dome.

"Gosh! Look at that!" Rami gasped. He stood transfixed with his eyes glued to that thrilling figure until he awakened to a thudding close of the door he left open. He slowly tiptoed back and went to his room and flung onto the couch.

He shook his head in disgust and leaned back in the couch contemplating what to do. While he was drowsing, lost in thought, a faint cough came out of the kitchen.

He rushed to the kitchen, fumbled the door open and peeped inside. Sheboun and his girl were sprawling on a bed with one end of the mattress tumbling down onto the littered kitchen floor. The pillows and the bed sheet were piling up on the floor. The girl's hair was disheveled and it cascaded down the corner of the bed.

"Sheb, Sheb, Sheboun" Rami called in a weary, choked voice. He almost lost his voice due to the drink and the cigarette smoke.

Sheboun groaned and turned on the other side and then groped around for the blanket.

"Sheboun, it is noon!" Rami whispered. "Sheboun, Sheboun."

"It is midday, come on wake up," he kept repeating.

"I heard you," Sheboun finally murmured.

"Get up, let's go!" Rami urged.

Sheboun eventually sat up on the bed, squinted at Rami and in a weary dry voice he said, "My shoes?"

Pointing to where the shoes were, Rami said, "There they are."

Sheboun stretched, yawned lazily and then said, "I need a damn cigarette!"

"We will get it on our way," Rami reassured.

The two boys eventually left the den and headed back home to the farm.

They took the back lane and sneaked into the compound and on their way to the workers' dorm, they bumped into a huge figure standing in front of them with his hands on his hips. It was the man in charge of the farm. The man glared at the boys for a moment and then in a soft laden voice he said, "Did you come back to pack up your bags?"

The boys stood still little unsteady on their feet and hung their heads in affirmation. They were tired and sleepy from the exhausting experience of the previous night.

After a while, Sheboun slowly raised his head and stuttered, "B-b-boss, w-w-we did not mean t-t-to….!"

"DIDN'T MEAN WHAT?" The man snarled. "Don't you explain to me? This sort of recklessness is out of place here!"

Out of the corner of his eye, Rami looked at Sheboun and whispered, "Shut up! Don't you stoke up the flame?"

After a long stinking rebuke the boss finally gave them a strong warning and let them get back to work.

For the next weeks, the boys were in the farm compound twenty-four seven. As days dragged on, life became duller and duller and Sheboun grew irritable. For more than two weeks, they suppressed the urge to visit the den and they were broke. Their workmates refused to lend them money. They tried all possible ways to get money, but all attempts were futile. One boring, hot Saturday around noon while Rami was busy feeding the chickens, Sheboun came rushing to him, with his face unusually bright, and whispered, "I have something good to say!"

Blushed with excitement, Rami eagerly searched Sheboun's face and said, "What is it?"

Sheboun gave a wry smile and whispered, "Here's a good catch for us and tonight we're going to feast!"

"Feast! A wonderful surprise! What kind of feast?" Rami asked excitedly.

"We're going to have some liquid refreshment in the den!" Sheboun replied.

Rami gave a short, ambivalent laugh and said, "How? We're skint!"

"Don't worry! Pundits will always find ways out!" Sheboun reassured brightly.

"Got some money?" Rami asked enthusiastically.

Sheboun glanced around and then nodding in the direction of the chicken he whispered, "You've all the money you need in these larks!"

"WHAT? You must be kidding!!" Rami surprised.

Sheboun slowly bolted the door behind and urged, "Come on pal; we must make it out of here before these stupid buggers wake!"

Rami reached to a bucket in a corner, rinsed his hands and then turned around and said, "What're you talking about? I think the heat made you hallucinate!"

"I'm serious! This is the only way to treat ourselves!" Sheboun insisted.

"Look Sheboun! This time the boss is going to kick us out! We cannot afford losing the job." Rami resisted.

"Don't worry we're not going to repeat what we did last time. We will come back before midnight!" Sheboun reassured.

"And what if they discover some of the chickens are missing?" Rami asked suspiciously.

"Aah!! Come on pal! Five or six chickens don't make any difference to a heard of five thousand heads! After all, no one even knows the exact number of the chickens in this farm!" Sheboun continued reassuringly.

"It would be foolhardy to trade stolen chickens for a drink!!" Rami reflected.

While the chickens were unwary feeding, the boys captured six of them and gagged their beaks with plastic tubes. And before everybody was awake, Sheboun smuggled them out with a carriage bike. Rami slipped out of the compound and took the back lane and caught up with Sheboun. They got on the bike and rode off their way to the *sin place*, Kadugli.

In less than an hour, they were already at the gate of Sheboun's favorite inn. They propped the bike at the gate and fetched two chickens along with them and entered the house.

The moment they entered the compound, they were greeted by an erotically pleasant mix of incense smell and an aroma of fresh coffee. An elaborate coffee ceremony was going on. Sheboun's girl and Sadri were chatting merrily over the coffee. Two men were sitting on the other end of the room drinking beer. It was early afternoon and the house was clam and tranquil.

Sheboun kissed his girl on both cheeks and then without a preamble, he said, "These *cage geese* might add spice to our feast!"

He handed the two chickens to Sadri and kissed her on the forehead and then he hurried towards the gate. Before he stepped out he glanced back and said, "Bitza make yourself at home! I won't be late!"

Rami joined Sadri and Didi for coffee.

"So you're Sheboun's best friend" Didi tried to confirm.

"I came to know him at work place!" Rami said.

"You don't live in Kadugli! I mean I have seen you here only twice!" she said.

"That's right!" Rami nodded in agreement.

"You live in……I mean your home town…" She hesitated.

"Here and there!" Rami replied.

"No fixed address!" She commented.

"A sort of……. actually, I'm from Alwadi town!" He laughed.

"That's cool! Not many people from your home town come here. What brought you here?" She said astonishingly.

"My aunt sent me to work at a poultry here around Juzran"

"So how do you find Kadugli?" She said.

"Getting used to it!" He told her.

She gave a broad smile exposing stunningly beautiful set of young white teeth and then she said, "You're already got used to it!"

21

Sadri poured coffee onto our cups and then she said, "I'm in the kitchen. I can see you're both into a big discussion!" Then she hauled herself up and moved towards the kitchen with her night gown sweeping the floor. Didi and Rami paused for a while and gazed at Sadri as she waddled her way towards the kitchen.

Rami turned around and then in low voice said, "She looks tired!"

"She put on more weight ever since she gave up smoking. Now better give up eating to lose weight! Poor lady!!" Didi commented.

Rami burst out laughing at what Didi said about Sadri.

Didi reached to a mirror on a table, stared at her image and shook her hair loose and then she said, "What's funny?"

"N-n-nothing!" Rami laughed.

Didi seemed more concerned about her appearance. She grabbed a comb and dragged it through her peroxided hair and then in a casual tone she said, "Sheboun said you're a gifted rabbaba player!"

Rami smiled and then said, "I only play it as a hobby! I like music."

She smiled back and nodded her head in agreement.

"I also try other musical instruments. Arkadi taught me how to play the guitar!" He added.

"Who's Arkadi?" She asked eagerly.

"He was a retired conductor…. a neighbor and a friend of the family. After school I used to spend most of the time practicing music with him," he explained.

After taking a long deep breathe in a low soft voice she said, "I have a half-sister, Julia who liked singing and dancing. I can still remember her singing when she was only eight years old. Actually her father taught her how to sing and dance. One day a man talked to her father. ….a week later the man came back and took Julia and her father along with him. Julia was only twelve years old then."

She sighed deeply and then continued, "They went far away to Gewaza. The last time I heard of her was when she sent me a letter. She said she was learning music!"

She paused for a moment and then continued her story as Rami listened silently.

"I used to live with my mother. One day my mother got sick! Very sick and then… and then……." She sobbed.

"I'm sorry!" He told her.

After wiping her tears, she continued, "After my mother's death I ran away and tramped the streets looking for job until I finally met Sheboun."

Their conversation was interrupted by a voice calling, "Two more beers!"

It was one of the men sitting in the far end of the room.

As Didi went to attend to the men, Rami took the opportunity to go to the toilet. While he was coming back from the toilet, he heard Didi shouting and swearing. He halted and stood out of sight in the corridor and saw one of the men grabbing Didi's hand and groping her. Didi was jerking and yelling!

After a while, he slipped into the room and coughed discreetly to announce his arrival. The man glared at Rami and laughed sarcastically and continued his business.

Didi patiently took the man's hand off her and said, "Keep your hands off me!"

Then Rami heard the other man taunting, "What's the matter with you lolita sitting there with a kid the size of my dick?"

Finally, the man patted her buttocks teasingly and let go of her.

They leered at her while she made her way to her table.

Didi went back to her table looking angry. "I hate these old cads!" She yelled.

"Relax! You don't need to get uptight about this!" Rami tried to mitigate.

She slumped down in her chair and breathed deeply before speaking again. After taking a long deep breath she stared at a clock on the wall and then grudged, "Sheboun's late! What the hell is he doing?"

Rami looked outside through the door expectantly and nodded in agreement, "Yeah he's a bit late!"

Didi hauled herself up and moved towards the doorway where a big cupboard was and then turned on a cassette player. She came back and started humming along with the music.

Then all of a sudden there was a loud bang outside. It was Sheboun opening the gate. The gate swung open as he thrust it with the front tire of his bike.

He propped the bike, entered the room and threw himself into a chair beside Didi.

He smiled at Rami and then said, "Time to quench!"

Rami smiled back and nodded his head in agreement. He divined their trick had paid off.

Sheboun unbuttoned his shirt and fanned himself to cool down. After a while, he rose up, yawned deeply and then grudged, "When's the food coming?......I'm starving!"

It was some time before they were greeted by a mouth-watering smell of roasted meat and fresh *gengeriba* bread floating out from the kitchen. Sadri was setting the table for dinner. She brought the food on a big tray with various rich plates on it. They gathered around the table excitedly. Sheboun inhaled the fresh flavor of a roasted chicken and then jokingly said, "May God keep the larks in their nests and Sadri's hearth at its best!" – A distortion of a local, traditional way of saying grace before a meal.

Rami laughed and gave a furtive glance at Sheboun and then muttered, *"What an irony!"*

Sheboun gave a wryly smile, grabbed a chicken drumstick and started biting it off greedily.

The gullible Sadri and Didi both laughed amusingly and dug their hands onto a plate of rice and started eating leisurely. Rami spat out a chewing gum and stuck it on the bottom of the table and then grabbed a loaf of *gengeriba* bread and started eating it with chicken soup.

It was an elaborate meal consisting of roasted chicken, chicken soup, rice and rolled loaves of *generiba* bread, a special Kaduglian cookery. Then they washed down the meal with one bottle of beer each.

After the meal, they took a table in a corner and ordered Sheboun's favorite drink, *Katikala*. As usual, the carousing commenced with *Katikala* and soda water and continued with beer. For the first few hours, they enjoyed a calm, festive atmosphere. Now it was late evening and the customers were pouring in and the hubbub of the bar life gradually began to grow. Bottles kept coming and the mood of the feast alternated between moments of dancing and drinking. Rami was savoring every sip of the drink.

This time, the setting was quite different. They were sitting in the main bar. The room was spacious and lively. Two bare tungsten bulbs dangled from the ceiling casting cones of light upon men who were drinking and raving at each other. The noise in the room was muted by a loud music echoing in all corners of the room. Cigarette smoke drifted and rolled in the beams and followed the men when they moved quickly. The room was getting warmer and dirtier as the night dragged on.

Two young bar maids in alcohol stained gray aprons were attending to the customers. The customers teased and flirted with the barmaids as they floated around. Sometimes the girls avoided the men and at times they laughed and sat on their laps and teased tantalizingly. That night, Didi was relieved. She had been on the day shift.

Sheboun studied Rami's face and said, "You have become proficient at the game!"

Flattered by the compliment Rami nodded his head in disbelief and then laughed ambivalently. The alcohol slowly took effect on him.

Around midnight one of the customers, the very man who had been chasing after Sheboun's girl, bumped into Sheboun's table, and started talking gibberish. He was as drunk as a skunk and his speech was slurred.

Sheboun stared up at the man and said, "To what do we owe the honor of your presence at our table!"

Sheboun was also drunk. The little berry-brown bottles grew in number on their table and they were still in a mood to continue drinking.

The man leaned forward, rested his hands on the table and then slurred, "Good kill!"

Sheboun gave a cynical smile and said, "Thank you!"

The man paused for a moment and then blathered, "Don't be selfish….you can't have a bar girl all to yourself! Learn to share the meat!"

Sheboun raised his head and with a grim face snapped, "What!!!"

With a gesture of despise on his face the man sneered, "Where the hell are you from?..... She's quite a meal for everyone hungry!"

Sheboun whirled around and snapped back, "And who the hell are you to pester around? And as for the girl she isn't that sort! She's mine!"

The man paused for a while and swore, "And since when inbred swines began to own girls in a bar!"

Sheboun stared at the man furiously and sneered, "And since when the rotting old cads began to desire tender meat?

The man flared his dark eyes and sneered, "Fuck you! You little inbred swine!"

Sheboun leaped to his feet and swore back loudly, "Fuck you too! You rotting old rascal!"

In frenzy violence, the man snatched a bottle of beer and hurled it at Sheboun.

Sheboun ducked and the bottled zoomed past his head and crashed into the wall shattering into pieces.

Sheboun leaped aside and drew a jackknife and darted towards the man.

The man whirled around and snatched a chair from the table across. However, he was stopped in tracks by one of the customers.

Didi and Rami rose up and rushed towards Sheboun and tried to stop him, but he shoved them aside and moved toward the man.

The Music stopped suddenly and a deafening silence fell in every corner of the room. Rami was consumed with fear when he saw tempers were getting frayed. He was terribly worried about Sheboun. Sheboun was very special to him not only as a friend, but as a brother and he couldn't bear seeing him in trouble.

Then all of a sudden, there was a voice crying out, "Can anyone tell me what the hell's going on here! Has everybody gone mad tonight?"

It was Sadri, she was accompanied by a tough looking man. The man waded into the fray and struggled to split the adversaries. Another man stepped in. Sheboun and his opponent were exchanging swear words as they were being hauled away into different directions.

Sadri stared at the two opponents angrily and yelled, "If you want to continue the fight, take it outside!"

The other customers just remained in their seats and watched to see what would come next. In discreet silence of all other men the man laughed. His laughter rang somehow childish. The other men by this time had begun to look at him askance, as if they wished to inquire what ailed him. Sheboun went back to his table while casting a look of heated scorn at his adversary. He grabbed his wallet from the table and from a distance he gestured for Rami to take Didi and go to the next room. Rami held Didi by her hand and they both stepped out to the corridor instead. After a while, Sheboun came out looking furious and told Rami to take the bike and leave. He reassured him that he would catch him up. He accompanied Rami to the gate, put his arm around Rami's shoulders and whispered, "I'll have some time with Didi lest that bastard disturb her again!"

After a brief argument, Rami finally got on the bike and rode off his way to the farm. The memory of the incident heavily weighed on his mind and he didn't feel the distance and the things around until he awoke to the faint squawks from the poultry.

It was post-midnight when he reached the farm and everybody was fast asleep. He quietly propped the bike and entered his room. He groped through the darkness towards his bed and lay down and closed his eyes contemplating.

After a while, he got out of his bed and went outside. He stood looking up at the stars. The stars flickered and went out in the pale cold winter sky. He yawned drowsily and went back to his room and lay down.

He awoke from a deep sleep to the sound of heavy knocks on the door. He hauled himself out of the bed and swayed outside giddily. His body was sore all over. He squinted into the sun and then looked around and saw his workmates gathering around the dining table. It was already noon. They stared at him and started murmuring as he passed by on his way to the bathroom. While Rami was coming back he was waylaid by one of the workmates.

"And, how're you, then?" The man asked with a sneer in his voice.

"Fine!" Rami nodded

"What about lunch?" He asked

"No, I really don't feel like eating" Rami replied.

"Sick?" He asked.

"No," Rami smiled faintly and then moved towards his room.

Rami entered the room and sprawled on his bed and then stared up at the old dirty ceiling and started muttering under his breath. After a while he heard footsteps outside of his room. Then he heard a voice saying, "Bitza, the boss wanted to see you!"

He knew the boss was up to something and an air of fear loomed up ahead of him. He sat up on his bed and pondered for a while over the boss's intention of calling him.

After a brief struggle with his conscience, he hauled himself out of the bed and muttered, "*It must be all about the stolen chicken....After all I didn't want to work here, and it was my aunt who got me into this shit. I want to learn music and not to cleanup chicken shit. I'm only seventeen and I have the whole world ahead of me. I want to be a great musician like Arkadi!*"

Consoling himself with this thought, Rami cared less about the boss. His fear diluted into a thin air and he went straightway to the boss.

The boss stared at Rami, pulled a wry face and then said, "Where's your friend?"

Rami rubbed his chin and looked away to avoid the man's eyes and remained silent.

Then he heard the boss saying, "The police were looking for you!"

Rami whirled around and then stuttered, "The police!"

A wave of shock swept over his body. He was confused and perplexed as to why the police were looking for him.

"This is a workplace and not a hideout for juvenile criminals!.......You should have been in jail with *him!*" continued the boss blatantly.

Paralyzed with fear, Rami muttered, "What the heck?.....*What happened to Sheboun?...And why did the boss wish me imprisonment?...........*"

The boss walked away and turned around and said, "All I can say to you is: pack up and disappear immediately!"

Strangely, Rami didn't feel crushed. He felt liberated instead. Now all he could think of was Sheboun. Suddenly, it dawned upon him that Sheboun was the reason why he was in the poultry.

Without a second thought, Rami went back to his room and packed up his effects. First, he was not sure where to go, but finally his thoughts turned to Sadri's bar. He had to find out about Sheboun. Lost in thought, Rami didn't feel the distance and soon he was at the notorious bar. The memory was so fresh that it seemed it was only few minutes ago that he left the bar.

Didi was surprised to see Rami. She looked pale and drawn. Rami could divine that something had seriously gone wrong.

She stared at him and said, "You're not supposed to be here!"

Rami held her hands and asked, "What do you mean?......Why am I not supposed to be here?"

Without replying to his question, she slowly sat on the edge of her chair, her arms hanging between her thighs and then in a low dry voice she said, "Sheboun is in jail!"

"Yeah I heard that! What happened?......Did the fight erupt again?" Rami said in a laden, curious voice.

She shook her head in disgust and said, "They were caught dealing marijuana!"

"WHAT?" Rami gasped. "What're you talking about?"

She took a long deep breathe and said, "After just you left, one of his acquaintances came in and talked to him and then they both went out. After a while, two men who were later identified as security men raided the house and arrested Sheboun and his fellow. They were caught red-handed!"

"I don't think Sheboun would do that so openly. It must have been a set-up!!" Rami denied sternly.

She bent down to shake a pebble out of her shoe and said, "Yeah, I think it was a ruse to put him in jail, but I also blame Sheboun for his recklessness!"

"Too bad!!" Rami nodded in disgust.

"Don't worry; prison is his home away from home!" She said bluntly and then removed a slip of paper tucked into her bra.

"This is what I managed to get when I went to the police department today in the morning," she said as she handed over the paper to Rami.

It was a quick note from Sheboun.

The note read:

Dear my prodigy,

I know how much you'll be missing me. It seems I will be behind bars for a while! Don't worry about me and don't ever think to visit me. I know you'll no longer be at the larks'. Go! ...Go wherever your destiny leads you. I'll find you wherever you are!

Sheboun.

Rami slowly slipped the paper into his pocket and held Didi by her arms and then said, "I have to go!"

He couldn't help, but he felt like he was abandoning his friend, leaving him behind. Heeding the message on the note, he decided to run away as far as possible.

Didi stared at Rami and hugged him tightly and said, "Take care! Stay in touch."

Rami sighed deeply and said, "of course I'll be in touch!"

He kissed her on forehead and left. As he left the house it was dusk. Rami pursued his way until being about to turn the corner by the meetinghouse. Then he looked back and saw the head of Didi still peeping after him with a melancholy air.

He was not quite sure where to go. Anyway, he just pushed his way towards the heart of the town with no clear destination in mind. While he was loitering in the streets, all of a sudden his attention was caught by a shop sign saying: *Sherooq Snack Bar.* Without a second thought, he just slid into the snack bar. He sat at a table in a corner, took out Sheboun's message and started gazing at it. Suddenly, he heard a voice saying, "How can I help you?" He slowly raised his head and looked left and right and said, "I want special *fatta.*" Then he continued studying Sheboun's message oblivious to the noise around until he awoke to the sound of a plate banging on his table.

Rami was not really sure why he was there. Although he hadn't eaten anything since the evening before, he didn't feel like eating or drinking. Lost in thought, he started chewing his food mechanically, as he continued gazing at the letter.

He outstayed all of the clients and soon he realized that he had no place to spend the night. He had money, but he had never been to hotels before.

One of the waiters came to his table and said, "It's time to close, can you pay the bill?"

Rami stared up at the waiter and nodded, "Sure!"

He settled the bill and asked the waiter if he knew anything about *Al-Sheruk* store, a tobacconist's, where Sheboun used to work before he came to the poultry. Rami had to see the tobacconist and break the news to him. That's what all he could do about Sheboun. The waiter told him that the store was about an hour's walk across a small ravine in the western outskirts. He warned him that it wouldn't be safe to walk alone, especially in late night hours. In spite of the possible dangers, Rami decided to take the short route across the ravine.

He had taken a dreary path darkened by all the gloomiest trees, which barely stood aside the narrow path. It scared him to think he was walking alone in late night hours. With lonely footsteps, he glanced fearfully behind him. His head being turned back, he passed a crook of the path and dragged across the ravine, and looking forward again, saw a hearth of fire ahead of him. He stood still astounded to see fire in the open air! The scene was so eerie that he argued with himself whether it was a hallucination or real fire. He pinched himself to make sure it was not hallucination! After a while, he heard a hubbub wafting towards him distantly. It was a very cold winter night and the bed of the ravine was dappled with pale moonlight. He walked forward with slow light steps until he finally halted to a loud laughter. He stood motionless holding his breath for a moment in an attempt to identify who those mysterious people would be. He was stuck in limbo. He neither could move ahead nor backward. While he was struggling with his conscience, he was startled by a deep voice saying, "Don't be scared! They are shepherds... they usually build fire to keep their flock warm!"

Rami whirled around and scanned the surrounding for the source of the voice. His terrified eyes rolled in every direction until he finally saw an eerie figure approaching him right from behind. Frozen with shock, he stared at the mysterious figure.

"You must not fear," the voice reassured without a preamble. "We shall soon set matters right."

It was a barrel-chested man with a shawl draped around his shoulders. In the pale moonlight, everything about him seemed dark and Rami couldn't make out his features. The man seemed to have been following Rami stealthily.

"I can see that you are shivering. It's a very cold night. Isn't it?" the man continued.

Rami stared at him for a moment and in a low ambivalent voice said, "It is not the cold which made me shiver."

"What, then?" the man laughed.

"It is fear!" Rami replied.

"Fear of what?......You don't need to be afraid!! Your friend will be ok!" he reassured ironically.

"Friend!!......Friend who? ......What are you talking about?......And who're you by the way?" Rami sent out a barrage of confused questions.

"Easy...... Easy kid!" the man tried to calm him down.

"*Is this for real or hallucination?*" Rami reflected.

The mysterious man approached the boy, put his arm across his shoulders and said, "I guess you're on your way to the tobacconist's...... I'm afraid you will not find him........... ."

"WHAT?" Rami whirled around. He was perplexed by the words as well as the tone of the speech.

31

"Aren't you?" he tried to confirm.

"Of course I'm, but how did you know that?" Rami enquired with a surprise.

The man gently took his hand off Rami's shoulders and said, "It's a long story!"

"*Indeed it's a long and interesting story!*" Rami whispered.

Once again the man rested his hand on Rami's left shoulder and said, "Come on let's push on!"

Rami slowly took the man's hand off his shoulder and said, "Push on!!..... Push on where?"

The man laughed throatily and said, "Trust me, all is ok!!......Now it's late night and you have nowhere to spend the night.........!"

Now it dawned upon Rami that the man had followed him with a purpose. But He was not sure of the man's intention. An atmosphere of uncertainty and confusion brooded over him. Since he had no choice but to follow him, he followed.

Heading towards the man's home they plunged into a deep conversation.

"You know the fanciest thing happened while I was waiting for my food in the same restaurant where you had your dinner," the man commenced his story without Rami's invitation.

Rami looked at him askance and said, "What was that?"

"I bumped into a mutual friend of mine and your father's. ......He instantly recognized you the moment you entered. He told me all about you....... You're just like your father .... You know they say: *The apple doesn't fall far from the tree*......." The man continued.

"You knew my father?" Rami interrupted him.

"Like an elder brother!" the man confirmed. "We grew up together."

Rami was both astounded and excited by the bizarre turnaround of events. Meeting this man added a new twist to his life. So many questions stored inside him now rushed forth. He was excited to know more about his father.

Immersed in a deep conversation, he didn't feel the distance and the things around until they finally halted at a massive iron gate of a gigantic compound. The man unlocked the gate and pushed it open. As they stepped in a dog began barking at them.

The man slowly bolted the gate and said, "Easy…...easy …… easy boy……we mean no harm!" The dog kept barking widely, but when he recognized the man, he leapt into his arms playfully almost knocking him over. Rami stepped aside and scanned the compound impulsively. In the pale moonlight he could only see a dim shape of a massive building overshadowing the surrounding.

"The original plan for this space was to have a large tile factory here…… but as you can see we haven't quite got there yet!" The man chuckled sheepishly while stroking the dog's head.

Rami turned around and faced the man and asked, "Does the house belong to you?"

The man turned around and faced the building and then said, "I renovated it a year ago and it was only recently that I rented it out to a friend of mine who wanted to establish a tile factory……the equipment is ready, but to get a license is an arduous process!"

When Rami heard this, his heart swelled with happiness. He felt assured that this man would help him get a steady job enabling him to resume his music classes.

The man let go of the dog and beckoned Rami to follow him. He walked Rami to a room on the far end of the compound. He pushed the door open and went inside. After groping around in the dark for a while, he finally lit a candle and asked Rami to get inside. When Rami got inside, pointing to the direction of a mattress spread on the floor, the man said, "There you sleep!" Then he wished Rami goodnight and slipped out of the room. Rami bolted the door and scanned the room for a while. In the candle light he could only see a dim outline of the room. On the far end of the room there were stacks of cans and a bunch of cement sacks and on the right corner there was a wide empty space where the mattress was spread and beside it was a water jerrycan.

After surveying the room, he turned around and cast his eyes to his shadow on the wall and then muttered a sigh of relief, "Finally, here I am!!" Then he moved towards the mattress and slowly removed his shoes and sprawled in a supine position. The thought of spending a night in an alien place scared him and to make things worse he couldn't fall asleep. The house reeked of leaking paint and moldering cement sacks.

The next morning he woke up to the sound of thudding knocks on the door.

When Rami came out, his host was busy surveying cracks in the compound wall. The man glanced around and then smiled, "how was the slumber?"

Rami smiled back and nodded, "Fine." Although in reality he had an uncomfortable sleep.

After a brief exchange, the man turned away and continued his business.

Rami glanced around and scanned the compound for a bathroom until finally his eyes came upon a small nondescript building standing on the right corner of the gate. Assuming it was the bathroom, he made his way towards it.

When he came out of the bathroom the man looked at him with a smiling face and said, "Ready for breakfast?"

Rami smiled back and nodded, "Yeah."

Then the man walked him to the kitchen. Over the breakfast table they had a deep prolonged conversation. It was the first time that Rami became overt and spoke his mind to a stranger.

With his mouthful of food and grease dripping down his chin the man muffled, "You didn't tell me your name?"

"Oh, yeah......I thought you knew my name!" Rami said with a smiling face. "Anyway, I'm Rami, but I'm known by Bitza!"

"Bitza?" the man laughed. "What's that supposed to mean?"

Rami smiled and said nothing.

They paused for a moment busy gobbling their sandwiches. When Rami finished his breakfast, he rubbed his mouth with a tissue paper and glanced up at the man and said, "You said you knew my father?"

There was a brief pause. Then the man rose from the table, walked up and down the kitchen for a minute. Finally he stopped at the kitchen table, and picked up a cigarette. He looked at Rami, then over towards the kitchen window. There was something serious in his eyes, something thoughtful. He lit the cigarette and turned away towards the window and commenced his story.

"Your father was a close friend of mine. We were actually in prison together. Our friendship helped see us through those tough times...... Your father was a brave man. Even after we came out, we stayed close. In fact the woman I'm married to was recommended to me by your father. It was him who first introduced me to her."

Rami just gazed at him in amazement as the man narrated his wonderful story.

Tijani, that was the name of the man, threw the cigarette through the window and turned around and said, "His memory lives on!"

Having completed his discussion about Rami's father, the man shifted his attention to Rami.

"It seems like you are a drop out!...... so what's your next move?" Tijani inquired.

Rami glanced up and shook his head. "I don't know...... I'm just drifting and hanging out!"

Tijani turned back at him, rested his hands on the kitchen table and then said, "Life is not like chess...... it's not like you can play another round, so make your decisions wisely."

Rami turned away, paused for a while and then said, "Well, actually I want to be a musician."

"A musician?" Tijani laughed. "You must be kidding!"

Rami looked at him and said, "That's my earnest wish!"

Tijani made a deep frown and then asked, "what kind of musician do you want be?"

Rami grinned. "How many kinds do you think there are?"

"Be serious," Tijani made his frown a little deeper.

Rami laughed, throwing his head back, and then looked at him. "I'm serious."

"Well, then, stop kidding around and answer a serious question. I mean, do you want to be a concert singer; you want to play on stages or what?" he enquired.

"No! I don't want to be a concert singer. That isn't what interests me. I mean singing isn't my interest." Rami continued. "I want to be a guitarist."

"A guitarist? ...... Doesn't all this take a lot of time? Can you make a living at it," Tijani frowned.

Rami turned back to him and half leaned, half sat, on the kitchen table and then said, "Everything takes time...... and well yes, sure, I can make a living at it. But what I don't seem to be able to make you understand is that it's the only thing I want to do."

"Well, you know people can't always do exactly what they want to do," Tijani laughed.

Rami stared at him defiantly and then said, "No I don't believe in that. I think people ought to do what they want to do, what else are they alive for?"

The man shot a sharp look at the boy and then snarled, "Don't get cute with me! You ought to think about your future!"

"I'm thinking about my future...... I think about it all the time." Rami affirmed.

"Then you have to go back to school." Tijani insisted.

Rami moved from the kitchen table to the window and then turned around to face the man and said, "That's a terrible idea!"

"Do you have a better idea?" Tijani laughed.

Rami just walked up and down the kitchen for a minute and then stopped at the kitchen table and picked up a cigarette pack. Looking at the man with a kind of defiance and put one between his lips and then said, "Do you mind?"

"You're smoking already." Tijani laughed.

Rami lit the cigarette and nodded, watching him through the smoke and then said, "I just wanted to see if I had the courage to smoke in front of you." He grinned and blew a great cloud of smoke to the ceiling.

Tijani shook his head in disgust and said, "That's rather daring!"

Rami looked at his cigarette amusingly and then said, "I bet you started smoking and drinking at my age."

Tijani didn't say anything but the truth was on his face, and he laughed. But now there was something very strained in his laugh.

"Let's cut the crap and get down to business...... I think you should go back to school. I will help you get a seat in a boarding school," Tijani promised.

Rami whirled at him and with an adamant voice said, "I would rather join the army than go back to school....... I don't care!"

"You must be crazy!" Tijani shouted.

There was a brief gloomy silence. Then Tijani continued. "What the hell do you want to go and join the army for?"

"I just told you!" Johny replied.

Tijani seeing that his protestation was leading nowhere, he flung out his arms in exasperation and left the kitchen.

Rami found his classes boring and meaningless while he was in his tenth standard and this made him hate school. Tijani used all his charm and logic to convince him to get back to school. Even though he loved and respected Tijani, it was impossible for him to be cajoled into this issue, since he felt that classes were a great hindrance to work towards his ambition of becoming a musician.

Over time, Rami's hatred of school deepened and he began to act out progressively, getting worse and violent. He went from teasing teachers and speaking out rudely to vandalizing school property. The school administration grew impatient with his persistent offences.

It was a Friday afternoon when Rami was summoned to appear before the faculty of the Al-Kubri High School to account for the alleged various misdemeanors. He was expelled from school a week ago and his father's best friend and now Rami's next of kin had called at the principal's office and confessed his perplexity about the boy. He appealed for leniency pleading with the school disciplinary committee to re-investigate the complaints made against the boy. Rami entered the faculty room suave and smiling. The committee members looked at him askance, as if they wished to ask him what ailed him. Tijani glared at the boy silently and shook his head in disgust.

The school principal peered with his spectacles resting on the bridge of his nose and then in a low but a laden voice said, "Do you know why you are here?"

Rami remained silent for a while, bit his lower lip and then in a polite voice said, "I want to come back to school!" This was a camouflage for the way he felt how he shamed his family. When the principal asked the accusers to state their respective charges against the boy, there was a divided opinion among them. The English teacher who was leading the pack of the accusers was very vocal in her disapproval of Rami's misbehavior. She sent a barrage of charges while fixing her accusing eyes on the boy. The charges were made with such a rancor and aggrievedness. Disorder, impertinence, and insubordination were among the offences named. Yet each instructor felt that it would be impertinent to really describe the real cause of the trouble, which lay in a sort of hysterically defiant manner. They all felt that the boy was terribly stubborn and seemingly made not the least attempt to conceal his bad behavior. The English teacher describing Rami's misbehavior in the classroom complained that once Rami when he had been making a synopsis of a paragraph at the blackboard; she had stepped to his side and attempted to guide his hand. Rami glared at her silently and jerked away her hand violently. The astonished woman could scarcely have been more hurt and embarrassed had he struck at her. The insult was so involuntary and definitely personal as to pass it off as a juvenile behavior. In

37

one way or another, he had made all his teachers, men and women alike, conscious of the same feeling of physical aversion. In one class, he habitually sat with his hand shading his eyes; in another he always looked out of the window during the lecturing; in another he made a running commentary on the teacher with humorous intent by taunting about the teacher's weight.

As the inquisition proceeded, one of the teachers repeated an impertinent remark of Rami's, and the principal asked Rami whether he thought that a courteous speech to make about a woman. Rami shrugged his shoulders slightly and his eyebrows twitched and then replied, "I don't know. I didn't mean to be polite or impolite, either. I guess it is a sort of way I have, of saying things regardless."

The principal asked him whether he didn't think that a way it would be well to get rid of that kind of behavior. Rami grinned and said he guessed so. When he was told that he could go, he bowed and went out. There was an element of contempt and mockery in his bow.

Some of the teachers, however, were disappointed by the committee's decision; especially his math teacher who voiced the feeling of the moderate teachers declaring there was something about Rami which none of them understood.

"I don't really believe that smile of his comes altogether from insolence." The teacher noted.

There was a complete silence. The teacher paused for a while and then continued, "There is something odd about the boy.... He is not strong for one thing. There is something seriously wrong about the fellow."

The math teacher had come to realize that, in looking at Rami, one saw only his white teeth and the forced animation of his eyes. One warm afternoon in the middle of the class, the boy had gone to sleep at his desk and his teacher had noted with amazement what a brown pale face it was; drawn and wrinkled like an old man's. The boy was twitching his dry lips even in his sleep.

The teacher left the trial room dissatisfied and unhappy; humiliated to have felt so vindictive toward a mere boy, to have uttered this feeling in cut term and to have set each other on, as it were, in the gruesome game of intemperate reproach.

Much to Rami's sympathizers' relief, after an arduous deliberation, the committee finally let the boy get back to school on a probationary basis.

Rami left the room and went down to Mushriq Concert Hall where he used to work as an usher during the weekends. The concert hall was famous for hosting popular bands from around the region. He tumbled down the street whistling and humming.

When he reached the concert hall the doors were not yet open. It was chilly outside, and he decided to go up the picture gallery. The gallery was always deserted at this hour. He was delighted to find no one in the gallery but the old guard, who sat at the corner, a newspaper on his knee, a black patch over one eye and the other closed. Rami possessed himself of the place and walked confidently up and down, scanning the posters on the wall while whistling under his breath. After a while, he sat down and lost himself. When he looked at his watch, it was after seven o'clock and he rose with a start and tumbled downstairs. It was time for him to report for duty.

When he reached the usher's dressing-room, two boys of about his age were there already, and he began excitedly to tumble into his uniform. It was one of the few that at all approached fitting, and he thought it very becoming, though he knew the tight, straight coat accentuated his narrow chest, about which he was exceedingly sensitive. He was always excited while he was dressed, twanging all over to the tuning of the strings and the preliminary flourishes of the horns in the music room; but tonight he seemed quite beside himself, and he teased and plagued the other boys until telling him that he was crazy. They put him down on the floor and sat on him.

Somewhat calmed by his suppression, Rami dashed out to the front of the house to seat the early comers. He was a model usher. Gracious and smiling he ran up and down the aisles. Nothing was too much trouble for him at the concert hall. He carried messages and brought programs as though it were his greatest pleasure in life, and all the people in his section thought him a charming boy feeling that he remembered and admired them. Beyond the practical matter of providing income, the concert hall brought him immense pleasure and instant gratification. As the house filled, he grew more and more vivacious and animated, and the color came to his cheeks and lips after a long lousy day at the school. It was very much as though it was a great reception and Rami were the host. Just as the musicians came out to take their places, his English teacher arrived with a check for the seat. It was an extraordinary coincidence that his English teacher, his arch-enemy, was sitting in his section. Rami was startled for a moment, and had the feeling of wanting to put her out.

"What business does she have here among all these fine people and in this special concert?" he whispered in disgust. Anyways, he looked at her and checked the ticket and said nothing. "The ticket had probably been sent to her out of kindness," he reflected as he put down a seat for her.

When the concert began Rami sank into one of the rear seats with a long sigh of relief, and lost himself. The first sight of the instruments seemed to free some hilarious spirit within him. He felt a sudden zest of life; the lights danced before his eyes and the concert hall blazed into an unimaginable splendor. When this beautiful singer came on, the fans rose to their feet and welcomed her with a thunderous applause. Rami felt like dashing to the bandstand, snatch a guitar and strum on it. At this moment Rami forgot even the nastiness of his teacher being there, and gave himself up to the peculiar intoxication such personages at the concert hall always had for him. The singer chanced to be a young beautiful girl by no means in her first youth. She had that indefinable air of achievement, that the world-shone upon her, which blinded Rami to any possible defects.

After the concert was over, Rami was often irritable and wretched. Tonight he was even more than usual restless. He had his feeling of not being able to let down of it and give up this delicious excitement which was the only thing that could be called living at all. During the last number he withdrew and after hastily changing his clothes in the dressing-room, he slipped out to the side door where the singers' car parked. Here he began pacing rapidly up and down the corridor waiting to see his favorite singer to come out. All the singers and the orchestra came out except for the young singer.

At last she came out accompanied by the conductor who helped her get into the car. Rami felt himself to go after her, but she was gone and there was no way for him to exchange glances with her. She only left the faint smell of her perfume floating in the air. Rami lingered for a few minutes to talk to one of the concert hall guards. After a brief exchange, he finally left the hall and slowly walked down of one of the side streets off the main road. It was around 3:00 am and a light drizzle was falling.

He had a long distance to cover until he was in his home. He approached it tonight with nerveless sense of defeat, the hopeless feeling of sinking back forever into the ugliness and commonness that he had always had when he came home.

The nearer he approached the house, the more absolutely unequal Rami felt to the sight of it: his ugly sleeping chamber, the cold bath-room with grimy, rusted zinc roof, the cracked mirror. He was so much later than usual that there would certainly be inquiries and bitter reproaches. Rami stopped short before the door. He felt that he could not be accosted by Tijani tonight. Tijani was already bitterly disappointed. For a proud and well-respected man such as Tijani, the situation was greatly disgraceful and embarrassing since he was forced to beg the school administration for leniency to let Rami get back to school.

When he reached home, he found the gate locked. He was cold and wet. He went around to the back of the house and tried one of the basement windows and luckily he found it open. He raised it cautiously and scrambled down the basement wall to the floor. There he stood, holding his breath, terrified by the noise he had made; but the floor above him was silent, and there was no creak on the stairs. He was horribly afraid of rats, so he did not try to sleep. He sat looking distrustfully at the dark, still terrified lest he might have awakened his uncle. That night Rami didn't sleep until daybreak.

The following Saturday was fine; the sodden September weather was broken by the last flash of a wet summer. Tijani was talking to a young man over a breakfast table. The young man happened to be his tenant. He was talking in a brisk businesslike tone. He was of a ruddy complexion, with a compressed, red mouth, and faded, near-sighted eyes, over which he wore thick spectacles. Rami went straight to the kitchen and found the maid cleaning the dishes. He made himself an egg sandwich and gobbled it down and then left the house.

Tijani was busy talking to his friend and Rami had the chance to sneak out of the house before Tijani could take any notice of him.

He left the house with his math book conspicuously under his arm. The moment het got out of the house, he boarded a car and went straight to meet a young man whom he got to know at the concert hall. The young man was a member of one of the music bands. The previous night he invited Rami to drop in for Saturday's afternoon rehearsals whenever he could. For more than five months Rami had spent every available spare time hanging about music clubs and concert halls, particularly the Hafil Concert Hall where he was admired as a model usher. He had won a place there not only because he was a model usher, but also because he was an aspiring young musician.

In fact, it was at the concert hall that Rami really lived. The rest was but a sleep and a forgetting. This was Rami's fairy tale, and it had for him all the allurement of a secret love. The moment he inhaled and tasted the gassy odor behind the scenes, he breathed like a prisoner set free, and felt within him the possibility of doing or saying splendidly, brilliant things. The moment the orchestra beat out the overture all stupid and ugly things slid from him.

Rami's obsession about music became a common gossip among his acquaintances and friends. His math teacher repeatedly pointed out that Rami's mind was perverted by a garish obsession about music.

41

It was an apt description of Rami's character. Indeed, the childhood music corrupted his youthful mind. He got what he wanted from music, any sort of music, from an orchestra to folk concert. He needed only the spark, the indescribable thrill that made his imagination the master of his senses, and all he could make plots and pictures enough of his own. All he wanted was to be in an atmosphere, float on the waves of it, to be carried out away from everything.

The teacher further noted that Rami found the school rooms more than ever repulsive; the bare floors and naked walls, the boring teachers and the monotonous classes. He couldn't bear to have the other pupils think, for a moment, that he took these people seriously. He had to convey to them that he considered it all trivia. He had autographs and pictures of all singers who came to the concert hall which he showed them to his classmates, telling them the most incredible stories of his familiarity with these people.

As Rami was on the verge of breaking down, another misfortune was waiting him at school. As it is said misfortune or misery does not come alone, but in company. So a series of misfortunes were in line for him. He was caught red-handed at mid-term examination. He had the despicable audacity to wage a fatal attack on the teacher concerned. The end result was, as expected, he was summarily expelled from school. Moreover, he was banned from the concert hall. In disappointment, Tijani asked the concert hall manager not to admit Rami to the concert hall. These came as a shock to the concert hall manager and the employees. Especially, the manager was vastly shocked. Rami was a model usher and it was an irreparable loss for the concert hall manager.

Strangely, Rami didn't feel crushed. Instead, he had a curious sense of relief, as though he had at last thrown down the gauntlet to the things in the corner. Now it was time for Rami to do things he had never done or thought to do in his life.

It was wonderfully simple game. Yet it was foolhardily a stupid one. The only thing that at all surprised Rami was his own courage, for he realized well enough that he had always been tormented by fear. An apprehensive fear that had been pulling the muscles of his body tighter and tighter. Until now, he could not remember a time when he had not been dreading something. Even when he was a little boy, it was always there behind him, or before, or on either side. There had always been the shadowed corner, the dark place into which he dared not to look, but from which something seemed always to be watching him and Rami would do things that were not pretty to watch or to hear.

Yet it was but a day since he had been sulking in the streets. Yesterday afternoon that he had been sent to the bank to deposit money, as usual. And this time he was in luck that he was instructed to leave the book to be balanced. There were about six thousand pounds in check, and nearly four thousand in banknotes. Rami quietly transferred the banknotes to his pocket. At the bank he had made out a new deposit slip. His nerves had been steady enough to permit of his returning to the office at the concert hall where he had finished his work and asked for a two-day break giving a perfectly plausible pretext. He cleverly exploited the school case to work in his favor. He lied to the concert hall manager that he was summoned to appear before the school discipline committee.

Rami knew that the bank book would not be returned before Monday or Tuesday. So there was no way the concert hall manager would learn about the theft before Monday. From the time he slipped the banknotes in his pocket until he boarded a bus bound to Dindir, a boarder city, he had not known a moment's hesitation.

He arrived in the city late evening. After loitering in the streets for some time he finally came down to one of the restaurants of the city. He took a table at a calm corner and ordered a roasted chicken. After enjoying the dinner, he decided to have some liquid refreshment and went to one of the lounge bars, a few minutes' walk from the restaurant. Although he was new to the place, he didn't feel estranged. The music of the orchestra wafted through the door to greet him. As he stepped into the thronged corridor, he sank back into one of the chairs and propped against the wall to get breath. He was brought back to life by the lights, the chatter, the perfumes, and the bewildering medley of the color. He went slowly about the corridor, the smoking rooms, reception rooms as though he were exploring the chambers of an enchanted palace, built and peopled for him alone. After surveying the house, he went back to the music lounge and sat down at a table near a window. He was not in the least abashed or lonely and he had no especial desire to meet or to know any of the people in the house. All he demanded was the right to look on and conjecture, to watch the pageant.

He found it hard to leave this beautiful place and to go to bed that night. So, he sat long watching the show. When he went to sleep, it was with the light turned on in his bedroom. He lay awake tossing and turning in the bed all night.

On Sunday morning the city was practically shrouded in dust. Rami breakfasted late, and in the afternoon he fell in with a wild boy from the city who said he had run down for a little flyer. The young man offered to show Rami the night side of the town, and the two boys went off together after dinner, not returning to the hotel until seven o'clock the next morning. They had started out in the confiding warmth of a beer of friendship, but their parting in Rami's lodging was singularly cool. The young man pulled himself together to make his bus, and Rami went to bed. The next day, he woke at two o'clock in the afternoon, very thirsty and dizzy. He dragged himself out of bed and went to the bathroom. After taking a cold, soothing shower, he dressed up and slipped out of the room feeling very hungry and headed towards the heart of the city. The city provided Rami with a perfect hideout and the stolen money furnished him with a temporary relish. Drinking and eating expensive food became a part of his daily life. The routine continued for several days. And it was only a matter of time before things would veer into a bumpy road.

On the thirteen's day of his arrival in the town, the concert hall theft scandal broke. The whole affair was exploited in the local newspapers. The newspapers exaggerated the whole affair wildly and bruited about for days. The incident was exploited with a wealth of detail which indicated that local news of sensational nature was at a low ebb. The concert hall announced that the boy's relatives and acquaintances had refunded the full amount of his theft, and that they had no intention of prosecuting. The rumor had reached that the boy had been seen in the town, and his relatives had gone there to find him and bring him home.

Rami had just come into a restaurant for dinner; he sank into a chair, weak in knees, and clasped his head in his hands. The grey monotony stretched before him in hopeless, unrelieved years. He had the old feeling that the orchestra had suddenly stopped, the sinking sensation that the play was over. The sweat broke out on his face, and he sprang to his feet, looking about him with a wide conscious smile, and winked at himself in the mirror.

He had no sooner entered the dining room and caught the measure of the music, than his remembrance was lightened by his old elastic power of claiming the moment, mounting with it, and finding it all sufficient. The glare and glitter about him, the mere scenic accessories had again, and for the last time, their old potency. And for the first time he drank his beer recklessly. He drummed a nervous accompaniment to the music and looked about him, telling himself over and over that it had paid. He doubted, more than ever, the existence of love and understanding in the people around him.

He reflected drowsily, to the swell of the music and the chill sweetness of his beer. He might have caught a bus and travelled far away to the border and ventured into the unknown. But the other side of the world had seemed too far away and too uncertain then. He could not have waited for it. His need had been too sharp. If he had to choose over again, he would do the same thing tomorrow. He looked affectionately about the dining room, now gilded with soft mist.

Rami was awakened the next morning by a painful throbbing in his head and feet. He had thrown himself across the bed without undressing, and had slept with his shoes on. His limbs and hands were heavy, and his tongue and throat were parched. There came upon him one of those fateful attacks of clear-headedness that never occurred. He lay still and closed his eyes and let the tide of realities wash over him.

The memory of his early childhood fell upon him like a deadweight. He had no more money left, and he knew now, more than ever before, that money was everything. The wall that stood between all he loathed and all he wanted. The thing was winding itself up. He had thought of that on his first day in the town, and even provided a way to snap the thread. It lay on the lamp table in front of him. He had got it last night. But the shiny metal hurt his eyes and he disliked the look of it. His fate was guiding him and no way to escape.

Rami rose and moved about with a painful effort, succumbing now and then to the attacks of nausea. The ground shook under his feet and yet somehow he was not afraid of anything. He was absolutely calm. Perhaps because he had looked into the dark corner and knew it was time to make the irrevocable step to the unknown. It was bad enough, what he saw there! But somehow not so bad as his long fear of it had been. He saw everything clearly now. The main road of his life was drawn with implacable precision and the terrible thought of the crooked road, a road along which he couldn't turn aside had overcome him. For half an hour he sat staring at the knife. But he told himself that this was not the way, so he tossed the knife aside and moved towards a table placed on the doorway. He picked up a bottle of coke and uncorked it. After taking few sips, he slowly slipped his right hand into his pocket and picked out a small plastic sack and on it was rat poison. Half an hour or so later, he was found lying on the ground in a supine position, his eyes were closed and thick foam was oozing out of his mouth.

THE END

45

Printed by Printforce, United Kingdom